Frankie: A Frog's Story

Joanne Randolph

alphabet soup™
an imprint of

WINDMILL BOOKS™
New York

For Deming, who loves anything that hops, slithers, flutters, or flies

Published in 2009 by Windmill Books, LLC
303 Park Avenue South, Suite # 1280, New York, NY 10010-3657

First Edition

Book Design and Illustrations by: Planman Technologies (India) Pvt. Ltd.

Publisher Cataloging Data

Randolph, Joanne
      Frankie : a frog's story / by Joanne Randolph.
p.   cm. – (Nature stories)
Summary: Frankie the bullfrog tells how he developed from an egg to a tadpole
to the biggest species of frog in the pond.
ISBN 978-1-60754-095-3 (lib.) – ISBN 978-1-60754-096-0 (pbk.)
ISBN 978-1-60754-097-7 (6-pack)
      1. Bullfrog—Juvenile fiction   [1. Bullfrog—Fiction   2. Frogs—Fiction   3. Tadpoles—Fiction
4. Metamorphosis—Fiction] I. Title II. Series
      [E]—dc22

Manufactured in the United States of America

Ribbit! That's frog for "Hello!" My name is Frankie and I am a bullfrog. There are lots of different kinds of frogs in the United States, but bullfrogs are the biggest. We're pretty loud, too. Have you ever been near a pond at night and heard a honking sound? That may have been me.

Being noisy is an important part of being a bullfrog. In fact, my mom and dad met by singing to each other near a pond they both liked.

My dad liked Mom's beautiful golden eyes. They knew they were a good match because they made each other so "hoppy!"

6

Lucky for me, Mom and Dad decided to start a family. My mom laid tons of eggs—and I mean tons! She laid about 20,000 eggs with me and my brothers and sisters inside. We floated together near the top of the pond for awhile.

After about four days of floating around, we all broke free from our eggs. We were tadpoles! That's what you call baby frogs. Boy, was that a scary time. It seemed like everything around us wanted to eat us! I played it safe and hid in some leaves in the water. I ate as much as I could, and I started to grow bigger.

9

Have you ever seen a tadpole? A tadpole looks a lot different than a frog. I bet you wouldn't even recognize me if you saw my baby pictures. I looked more like a tiny fish than the handsome young frog you see today. When you look at pictures of yourself as a baby, you probably look a lot different in your baby pictures, too.

I swam around in the pond for quite awhile. I was busy eating and growing. Strange things started to happen. I started to grow legs, and my tail and gills started to disappear. Gills were the parts that helped me breathe under water, just like a fish. But I was turning into a froglet so I didn't need gills anymore.

One day, my tail went away. That was a big day for me! It was time for me to hop out of the pond for good. Have you ever tried something new? Did you feel a little scared? Well, when I hopped out of the water for the first time, I was a little afraid. I had been underwater for so long. Would I know what to do?

Guess what happened when I got out of the pond! My froggie instincts kicked right in! Instincts are those feelings that tell you what you should do, even when you aren't really sure. When I saw that dragonfly moving, before I even knew what was happening, my tongue shot out of my mouth. Snap! Gulp! I had just had my first meal as a frog.

I don't know about you and your friends, but my bullfrog buddies and I are not picky eaters! We'll eat just about anything that is not too big. I eat bugs, fish, snakes, and even birds. My uncle even ate a duck once. Now that's hungry!

19

Bullfrogs aren't the only hungry creatures around the pond, though. If I'm not careful, herons, raccoons, snakes, or other animals might try to have me for lunch! But they better watch out! I can jump a long way to escape. And I don't really taste very good anyway.

Now I'm getting ready to start a family of my own. I have been practicing my singing and I really hope I find a girl who has beautiful golden eyes just like my mom! So I'll say "Ribbit!" for now. That's frog for "Good-bye," too!

For more great fiction and nonfiction,
go to windmillbooks.com.